Susan LaBarre
Janine Nicholson

Dr. Mark's
MY BODY, MY BUDDY Series

THE CHEW CHEW POOP PEE EXPRESS

A Magical Journey Through Our Digestive System

TO PARENTS AND TEACHERS

This series celebrates the body as a lifelong buddy, to help children understand and value the systems that keep us healthy. Kids often ask questions about how things work, but they can't see the inner workings of their bodies.

The warm and friendly Dr. Mark helps them visualize what is going on inside and make the connection between what they do and how they feel.

Digestion can be a sensitive subject for some families. Many adults are embarrassed about bathroom words such as poop and pee. But kids love those words and enjoy provoking the grownups' discomfort by using them in public.

Digestion is an everyday activity, yet even some adults don't understand how food gets from one end to the other. It is our desire to make learning about the body fun, educational, and inspiring. The illustrations are engaging and funny... appealing to the adult sense of humor and gross enough to please the kids.

We hope you enjoy reading the Chew Chew Poop Pee Express as much as we enjoyed writing it.

Susan LaBarre and Janine Nicholson

"What brings you and Harry in today, Mrs. Doohickey?"

"Dr. Mark, Harry has a terrible stomach ache and diarrhea."

"Let's find out what's going on. Harry, little man, what have you been putting in there?" asked Dr. Mark.

Harry moaned, "Daddy took me to the fair yesterday, and I had a corndog and an ice cream cone."

"Sounds yummy!" said Dr. Mark.

Harry went on, "And half a pizza... and french fries... and 2 sodas... and popcorn... oh, and cotton candy!"

OOOH!

"Oooh! Now we know why your tummy hurts." Dr. Mark explained. "Too much junk food can upset your stomach. And then your food doesn't move smoothly down your digestive tract."

"There's a track in my tummy?" asked Harry, amazed. "Like a train track?"

"Sort of." laughed Dr. Mark.

"You know how trains travel from one place to another... making stops along the way to pick up and drop off passengers?"

"Yeah!" exclaimed Harry, excited. "The engine makes that choo choo sound as it rides down the track. So cool!"

"And," continued Harry, "the engineer blows the whistle at each station and when he goes through tunnels."

"WHOOO, WHOOO!"

Dr. Mark replied, "Harry, your digestive tract carries your food and drinks on a journey through your body. And it makes different stops along the way. Then the food and drinks get off at the last stop as poop and pee."

"My food becomes poop?" gasped Harry. "Ewwwwww! Pizza poop. And potato poop? Broccoli poop... yuk!"

Dr. Mark assured Harry, "Imagine your poop and pee as the leftovers that get thrown away by your body after it digests your food.

Your toilet is like a waste basket for your body's garbage."

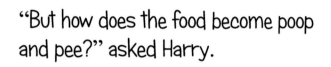

"But how does the food become poop and pee?" asked Harry.

"Excellent question, young man. Let's follow the journey as the food and drinks travel through your body."

JOURNEY THROUGH YOUR BODY

STRAIGHT AHEAD

"Think of it as a train trip with your food as the train," began Dr. Mark. "Your mouth is the first station. All your food and drinks board there."

Harry wondered, "How does the train move? Is there an engineer?"

"Oh," said Dr. Mark, "your BODY is the engineer and it knows the way – all the stations – and the final stop."

"The POOP and the PEE!" Harry announced helpfully.

"Yes, Harry, the poop and the pee.

Don't worry, we'll get to them at the end!"

Dr. Mark pointed to Harry's mouth as he explained the first stop.

"You use your mouth to chew your food and swallow your drink. **Saliva** (or spit) boards the train to help break down your food. Your teeth mash the food into tiny pieces.

Then your tongue can push it down the tract when you swallow. You have to chew your food really well so it slides down easily."

"Chew and chew and chew... until it's all mush."

"OK, so I swallow my mushed up food. Now what?" asked Harry.

Dr. Mark pointed to Harry's neck. "The food goes through the **esophagus**, which is a tunnel through your neck and chest."

Harry's eyes grew big with excitement. "Are there lights in my tunnel?"

"No, but you have little muscles that move your chew chew train through the tunnel to the next stop – your **stomach**." Dr. Mark pointed to Harry's belly.

Dr. Mark continued, "At the stomach station, some passengers get off and some get on – and some stay on the train."

"Who gets off?" Harry asked.

"Bubbles!" Dr. Mark answered. "We usually swallow some air when we eat and drink. The air isn't needed for digestion, so it's sent back up the tract as *gas*. We call that a burp."

"Ohhh – burps are way cool! Wanna see me burp, Dr. Mark?"

BuUuUURRP!

HARRY. THAT'S NOT NICE!

"You're very talented, Harry," grinned Dr. Mark.

"Who else gets off at the stomach station?" asked Harry.

"**Vomit**. Sometimes if you eat more than your stomach can hold or if your stomach doesn't like the food you're eating, it throws it back up through the esophagus."

"You mean puke?" Harry gagged.

"Puke stinks! I don't like to throw up. Why does it smell so bad?"

Dr. Mark explained, "Stinky **acids** board the stomach station to make your mushy food even mushier. When the acids mix with the food, the food becomes stinky."

"What if I DON'T WANT to vomit?" Harry protested. " Can I stop it?"

"Nope," the doctor answered. "When your body needs to vomit, it will do it, no matter how hard you try to hold it in... otherwise, you'd explode!"

"My mommy wouldn't want to clean up THAT mess."

"Your body protects you by making sure all your systems are working," continued Dr. Mark.
"When you feel sick, that's your body's way of making you rest so it can heal itself from bad germs or too much food."

"My body heals itself?"

"Your body naturally knows what to do – with help from your cool buddy Dr. Mark, of course!"

"What else happens in the stomach?" asked Harry.

"When all the food is mushy, the train moves it to the next station – your **small intestine**."

"It's a long, narrow, zig-zaggy food processing factory.

That's where the really exciting action happens! Passengers called **enzymes** come on board and send the **nutrients** from the fruit, veggies, meat and bread you ate into your **bloodstream**."

Harry's eyes grew wide.

"What's a NEW TREAT?"

"Nu-tri-ent," corrected Dr. Mark. That's the healthy stuff in your food that actually feeds your body." Dr. Mark added, "Everything else is waste."

"Waste?" giggled Harry.

"You mean POOP and PEE!"

"You have a one-track mind, Harry," grinned Dr. Mark.

Mommy wasn't amused.

"As nutrients flow through your bloodstream, your body uses them as **fuel** so you can grow and play," explained Dr. Mark.

"But, Harry, there's only so much fuel your body can burn. If you eat more than your body needs, that extra fuel is stored around your body as fat."

"All bodies need fat to keep them warm and to store fuel for later. But TOO much body fat is unhealthy. It makes your heart work harder.

That's why it's important to limit your sweets and greasy foods."

Hoping to stop talking about healthy food, Harry asked, "Where does the train go next?"

Dr. Mark continued. "The next stop is the **large intestine** (or **colon**).

Trillions of happy, hungry **bacteria** throw a farewell party for the food by eating all the leftovers your body can't use."

"But isn't it all stinky by now? It must taste awful. Yuk!" gagged Harry.

"The bacteria love the stinky taste just like some people like spicy food," said Dr. Mark. "The bacteria eat and eat and eat."

"They don't stop until ALL the leftover mush is eaten."

Dr. Mark continued, "Meanwhile, the liquid is funneled out into the bloodstream where it flows to your **kidneys**. As the liquids drain, the food mush gets drier and firmer until it clumps into a bunch of big, brown blobs ready to leave the station."

"Big, brown blobs?
That sounds like... like..."

"Yep," agreed Dr. Mark. "As each load fills up, it gets dumped into a storage station called the **rectum**.

When you feel like you've got to poop, it's because your rectum is full. Then you let it go through your **anus** into your toilet bowl."

Harry got excited, but mommy hid behind her chair.

"Uranus! That's a planet. We learned about it in school."

"No, Harry, replied Dr. Mark. "The word is ANUS. It is the hole between your butt cheeks that allows the **feces** to come out."

"Feces?" Harry was again puzzled.

"That's the scientific word for poop," explained Dr. Mark.

"I like POOP better," giggled Harry.

"We know you do, Harry. The point is – when you let go, it's the final stop."

"Bombs away, Dr. Mark!"

"Dr. Mark, why are some poops big and some small?"

"If you eat food that contains fiber, your poop will be larger, softer and easier to push out. Foods with lots of fiber include oatmeal, fruits, veggies and beans."

"Beans!!
They make you fart!"

"Farts are just gas bubbles made by the bacteria as they digest the food in your colon. Remember how your stomach got rid of gas bubbles by burping? Your colon gets rid of gas bubbles by farting. Doctors call that **flatulence**."

HAHA HA
HA
HA
HAHA
HA
HA

"And kids call them farts!"

Dr. Mark pointed out, "Some foods are harder to digest and that makes more gas bubbles. Cabbage, broccoli, cauliflower and beans are gassy foods."

"I made stinky farts this morning when I had diarrhea! Why is diarrhea wet?"

"Well, Harry, when the bacteria don't like the food or if nasty germs crash the party, the poop moves so fast there's not enough time for all the liquids to drain. So your poop stays wet and comes out as diarrhea."

"I'm confused, Dr. Mark. How come farts stink and burps don't?"

"Burp bubbles haven't yet mixed with the stinky acids in your stomach, so there's no odor."

"Dr. Mark, what about pee?"

"Harry, the liquids from your colon make a field trip through your bloodstream to your kidneys. Your kidneys filter liquid waste from the blood and send it to your **bladder**, which is another storage station."

"Doctors call this warm, yellow liquid **urine**. When your bladder gets full, you feel like you have to **urinate** or pee.

When you let go, the pee exits through its own tiny tunnel into the toilet."

"And that's the last stop. Everyone out!"

"And... the Chew Chew Poop Pee Express completes its journey," concludes Dr. Mark.

"Cool, Huh!"

"Wow! My own train set, inside my body."

"Remember, Harry – your body is your BUDDY. Your best buddy for your whole life. So if you love it and take good care of it, it will take care of YOU. What you eat and drink makes a BIG difference in how your body feels and how much energy you have."

"So eat healthy food and keep your `best bud` happy."

"That was an awesome story, Dr. Mark!"

Mrs. Doohickey breathed a sigh of relief and agreed, "Good job, Dr. Mark!"

"That IS my job – helping you take good care of yourself, Harry."

"... and I LOVE my job!"

As Harry and his mom were leaving the office, Dr. Mark overheard Harry asking his mother...

"Mommy, can we have broccoli and beans for dinner tonight?"

THE CHEW CHEW POOP PEE EXPRESS

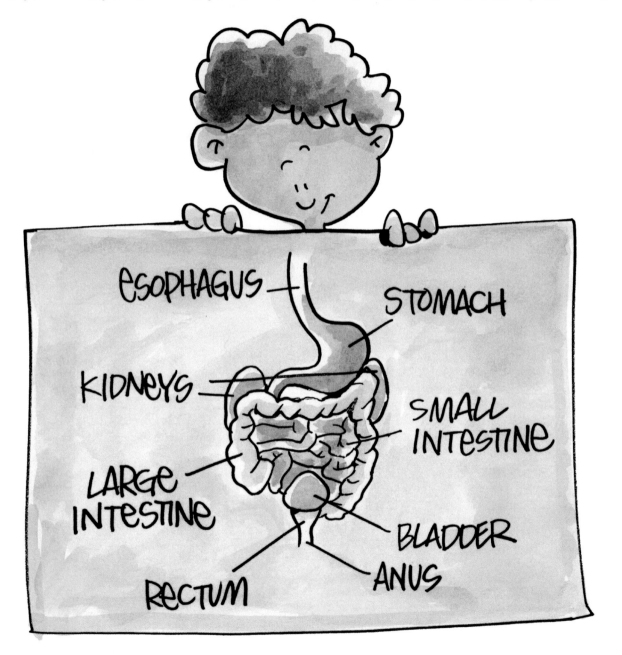

WHO'S WHO
ON THE CHEW CHEW POOP PEE EXPRESS

Susan LaBarre

A marketing and design professional, Susan has spent the last 20 years writing for and teaching technical and public audiences. Susan invented the Chew Chew express while consulting for the real life Dr. Mark. Her love of satire infuses this book.

Janine Nicholson

Having designed and taught innovative science curricula in public schools for 26 years, Janine has carefully steered this wild Chew Chew into an age-appropriate, fast paced, educational adventure. Janine works to sustain our natural resources for future generations.

Dr. Mark Larimer

Dr. Mark has been a medical doctor for 25 years. He most recently practiced family medicine in Raleigh, N.C. His whimsical personality, commitment to mind-body-spirit wellness, and extensive medical knowledge provides both the inspiration and subject matter for this book.

Jim Hunt

All our wonderful, whimsical illustrations were created by artist Jim Hunt.

Visit Jim at www.acartoonist.com.

Visit us at... ChewChewpoopeexpress.Com

Published in the United States.

HeartPath
Press

Made in United States
North Haven, CT
04 February 2022